Harriet
the Hamster
Fairy

For Leandro D'Olivera with my love

Special thanks to
Sue Mongredien

No part of this work may be reproduced, stored in a retrieval system,
or transmitted in any form or by any means, electronic, mechanical,
photocopying, recording, or otherwise, without written permission of
the publisher. For information regarding permission, write to Rainbow
Magic Limited c/o HIT Entertainment, 830 South Greenville
Avenue, Allen, TX 75002-3320.

ISBN-10: 0-545-04188-0
ISBN-13: 978-0-545-04188-1

12 11 10 9 8 7 6 5 4 3 2   9 10 11 12 13/0

Printed in the U.S.A.

First Scholastic printing, May 2008

Harriet
the Hamster
Fairy

by Daisy Meadows
illustrated by Georgie Ripper

SCHOLASTIC INC.

New York   Toronto   London   Auckland   Sydney
Mexico City   New Delhi   Hong Kong   Buenos Aires

Fairies with their pets I see
and yet no pet has chosen me!
So I will get some of my own
to share my perfect frosty home.

This spell I cast, its aim is clear:
to bring the magic pets straight here.
The Pet Fairies soon will see
their seven pets living with me!

Contents

Hamster-Sitting

"Here we go," Kirsty Tate said to her best friend, Rachel Walker. She turned the key in the back door of her neighbors' house. "Nibbles! Time for breakfast!" she called as the door swung open. "Just wait until you see him," she said to Rachel with a grin. "He's adorable. I love hamster-sitting!"

Kirsty's neighbor, Jamie Cooper, had asked Kirsty to feed Nibbles (his little orange-and-white hamster) while he and his parents were on vacation. She had said yes right away!

"We just need to fill up his food and water dishes," Kirsty told Rachel. "And if we're lucky, he might eat sunflower seeds out of our hands!"

"How cute!" Rachel said. "Where's his cage?"

"Over here," Kirsty replied, heading into the living room.

Excitement bubbled up inside Rachel as she followed her friend. They were going to see another pet after all. Over the last few days, she and Kirsty had shared some amazing pet adventures!

Rachel was staying with Kirsty's family for a whole week. On the very first day of her visit, the two girls had met the Pet Fairies! The fairies had asked Rachel and Kirsty for help. Jack Frost had wanted a pet of his own, but in Fairyland, pets choose their owners. None of them had chosen Jack Frost! He had been so annoyed that he had stolen the Pet Fairies' magical pets. Luckily, the pets had all escaped from Jack Frost into the human world. But now they were lost!

Rachel and Kirsty were determined to help the Pet Fairies find the magic pets before Jack Frost's goblins did. So far, the girls had found four: Shimmer the kitten, Misty the bunny, Sparky the guinea pig, and Sunny the puppy. But there were still three pets missing!

Kirsty led Rachel across the living room to the table with the hamster cage on top. But as soon as the girls reached it, they knew that something was wrong. The cage door was wide open!

"Oh, no!" Kirsty cried. "Don't tell me that Nibbles escaped on my very first day of watching him!" She carefully put her hand into the cage and searched

through the wood shavings and shredded newspaper for the little hamster, but it was too late. The cage was empty.

Kirsty and Rachel began searching everywhere they could think of. They looked under the table, around all the chairs, and behind the television. But there was no sign of Jamie's hamster.

"Nibbles!" Rachel called, picking up the hamster's food bowl and rattling it. "Nibbles, come have something to eat."

"Jamie's going to be so upset if he comes home and Nibbles is missing," Kirsty said. "Nibbles! Where are you?"

"He could be anywhere in the house," Rachel said. "Come on, let's try another room."

Kirsty nodded, and the girls headed out of the living room. But just as they reached the door, Kirsty spotted something. "Rachel, look!" she cried, bending down to examine the carpet.

She picked up a stray wood shaving
and held it up for her friend to see.
"A clue!"

"It must have been stuck to one of
Nibbles's feet when he climbed out
of the cage," Rachel guessed. "Look,
there's another one by the doorway.
And another!"

The two girls followed the trail of
wood shavings out into the hall. There,

8

they began searching around the coat rack and the side table.

Kirsty picked up the mail from the doormat and noticed that some of the envelopes were shredded. "Look!" she exclaimed. "Someone's been tearing up the mail!" Then she smiled as she realized what had happened. "Hamsters shred paper to make nests, don't they?" she asked. "I think Nibbles must have started trying to make a nest here!" She giggled

as she put the letters on the table. "Where did he go next, I wonder?"

"This way," Rachel said as she spotted a few pieces of shredded paper near the kitchen. "Come on!"

In the kitchen, the girls peered under the table and chairs, but there was no small, furry hamster in sight.

"Someone's been nibbling this fruit," Kirsty said, picking up an apple from the fruit bowl. Tiny teeth had chewed through the peel in a few places. "Nibbles must have stopped here for a snack." Then she frowned. "How did

he get up onto the kitchen counter, though?"

Rachel pointed at a nearby curtain. "Hamsters have strong claws," she pointed out. "I bet Nibbles climbed up the curtain to get onto the counter." She grinned, imagining it. "Nibbles is smart, isn't he?"

"Yes," Kirsty agreed, scanning the kitchen, hoping to spot a flash of orange-and-white fur. "But he's not here anymore. We'd better keep looking."

Rachel suddenly froze on the spot. "Sssh!" she whispered to Kirsty, putting a finger to her lips. "What's that noise?"

Both girls stood still and listened carefully. They could just hear a faint scratching sound coming from the hallway.

Kirsty grinned at Rachel. "Phew! It must be Nibbles scratching," she said. "All we need to do is follow that sound, and it should lead us straight to one adventurous hamster!"

The girls tiptoed out of the kitchen in the direction of the noise. The scratching seemed to be getting louder as they walked by the closet under the stairs.

"Nibbles, I'm coming to get you!" Kirsty giggled. She stepped forward to open the closet door, but before she could reach it, the door swung open by itself — and out jumped one of Jack Frost's green goblins!

Harriet Drops In

"Oh!" Kirsty gasped as the goblin laughed, charged out of the closet, and ran up the stairs.

Before either girl could say a word, a second goblin popped his head over the railing and stuck his tongue out at them!

Kirsty and Rachel glanced at each other in alarm.

Goblins in the Coopers' house could only mean one thing!

"There must be a fairy pet nearby," Rachel whispered, her heart thumping.

"Yes, and we have to find it before the goblins do!" Kirsty added, her eyes darting back and forth.

"Go away!" came a shout from upstairs.

Rachel and Kirsty both looked up. Now there were three goblins peering over the railing!

"We won't go away," Kirsty said, putting her hands on her hips. "We've come to feed Jamie's hamster. We're supposed to be here!"

The goblins all burst out laughing. "But isn't the hamster missing?" one of them managed to say between chuckles.

"Guess what? We let it out!" another one cried.

"What did you do that for?" Kirsty asked, crossing her arms.

"So that the pesky fairy hamster would come to the rescue, of course," the third goblin replied. "And when it does, we'll catch it and take it back to Jack Frost!"

Rachel frowned. "So you've set a trap for the magic hamster?" she asked. "That's horrible!"

"Well, if the fairy hamster does come, we'll find it first," Kirsty said, with a determined look on her face. "We'll give it back to Harriet the Hamster Fairy!"

"Not a chance," shouted the first goblin. Then all three goblins disappeared, and the girls could hear their big goblin feet thundering up the stairs.

Kirsty groaned. "This house is so big — it has three stories, a basement, *and* an attic! How are we ever going to find two little hamsters before those sneaky goblins do?"

"If there *are* two hamsters," Rachel reminded her. "The magic hamster might not have come to Nibbles's rescue yet."

Out of the corner of her eye, Kirsty suddenly spotted a sparkling red light in the living room. Curiously, she pushed open the door to see what was happening inside. "I think the magic hamster *is* here, Rachel," she said, her eyes wide as she gazed around.

Both girls stood in the doorway, staring at the room before them. It didn't look anything like it had a few minutes earlier! The wool rug had become a heap of wood shavings and shredded newspaper. Hamster toys were scattered

everywhere, and a mini-maze and two large exercise wheels were strewn across the floor. There were even bowls of nuts and seeds all over.

"Look!" Kirsty said. "This is hamster heaven!"

Rachel nodded. "This is definitely pet fairy magic in action," she said with a grin.

"We'd better find the magic hamster before the goblins do!" Kirsty pointed out.

Rachel peeked into the mini-maze. "With a little bit of luck, Nibbles will come scurrying in here any second," she said. "I mean, what hamster could resist all this?" As she turned to look around, her gaze fell upon the couch and she bit her lip in excitement. "Kirsty," she said quietly, so she wouldn't scare the little pet. "There's Nibbles!"

Kirsty looked where Rachel was pointing and saw an orange-and-white hamster sitting on a cushion. She stepped a little closer, to get a better look at him.

"That isn't Nibbles," she told Rachel.
"Which means it must be —"

But before she could say another word,
the hamster twitched its nose. A bright
shower of glittering red sparkles swirled
through the air. When the
fairy dust cleared,
the girls could see
a clear plastic
tube spiraling
down from
the couch
to the carpet.

The hamster
immediately
jumped into the
tube and started
scampering through
the spiral.

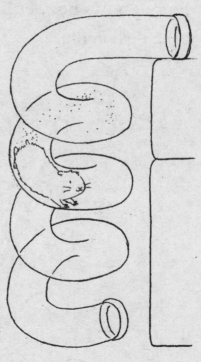

Kirsty laughed. "No," she said, "that's definitely not Nibbles. It has to be the magic hamster!"

Rachel smiled as the fairy pet scurried busily down through the plastic tube. "Do you think Harriet the Hamster Fairy knows her pet is here?" she asked excitedly.

Before Kirsty could reply, both girls heard a breathless voice cry, "Wheee!" behind them. They turned just in time to see a big black cloud of soot billowing out of the fireplace. As the dust settled, Kirsty and Rachel both grinned. There on the hearth, covered from head to toe in soot, was a tiny fairy!

Twinkle, Twinkle, Little Hamster

The fairy sneezed three times, blinked,
and waved a sooty wand over herself.
A bright stream of red sparkles shot out
of the wand and whizzed around her.
The soot disappeared in an instant!
"That's better," she said cheerfully,
and gave the girls a huge smile.
"Hello, again!"

Now that she was free of soot, the girls could see that Harriet the Hamster Fairy was wearing a light blue dress and sparkly red shoes. A glittery red flower hung on a chain around her neck, while another decorated the headband in her short blond hair.

"Hello, Harriet," Kirsty said, smiling at

the little fairy. "We were just wondering if you were nearby."

"And here I am!" Harriet said, smiling back. "I had a feeling that Twinkle, my pet, was somewhere around here."

"She is," Rachel said eagerly, "but there are three goblins here, too! We just saw them heading upstairs."

"They're awful," Harriet said, fluttering up into the air, "but I'm glad Twinkle's here. Where is she?"

"She's just about to come out of that spiral tube," Kirsty said, pointing at it with a grin.

Right on cue, Twinkle emerged. As soon as she saw Harriet, the hamster shrank to fairy-size and scampered joyfully up into the air. Rachel and Kirsty watched in delight as the tiny magic hamster scurried toward her fairy friend.

"Just what I was looking for!" a voice cackled.

Rachel and Kirsty spun around to see a goblin pop up from behind the couch. He had a horrible smirk on his face!

The goblin jumped quickly over the couch, grabbed the tiny pet out of the air, and ran out of the living room and up the stairs.

"Oh, no!" Rachel cried. "That goblin must have snuck back downstairs, looking for Twinkle. And now he's got her!"

"Quick, let's fly after him!" Harriet suggested, waving her wand and turning both girls into fairies.

She zoomed out of the living room,
leaving glittering red fairy
dust shimmering in the
air behind her. Kirsty
and Rachel
followed using
their delicate,
shining wings.

   As the three
friends flew
upstairs, they
could see the
goblins standing
on the next
flight of stairs,
which led to the top
floors of the house.
But when they spotted
fairies coming toward

them, the goblins turned and ran up the stairs. "Keep going!" Harriet cried, beating her wings even faster as she zoomed ahead. "Let's hide in here!" the girls heard a goblin shout as they reached the top of the second flight of stairs. They were just in time to see a goblin disappear through a doorway. "That's Jamie's bedroom," Kirsty whispered, coming to a

stop. "And it's not very big. There can't be too many hiding places in there."

"If we're girls again, it'll be easier for us to take Twinkle from the goblins," Rachel pointed out. "Could you use your magic to turn us back, Harriet?"

"Of course," Harriet said. She waved her wand again, and sparkling red fairy dust tumbled all over Kirsty and Rachel. "There,"

she said as the girls quickly grew back to their normal size. "Now, let's go hamster hunting!"

Rachel and Kirsty crept into Jamie's bedroom, while Harriet hovered behind them. There was a bed, a closet, a dresser, and a big toy box, but no goblins in sight.

Rachel headed straight for the toy box and lifted the lid. There were no goblins inside, just a collection of Jamie's plastic dinosaurs, toy cars, and some colorful rubber snakes.

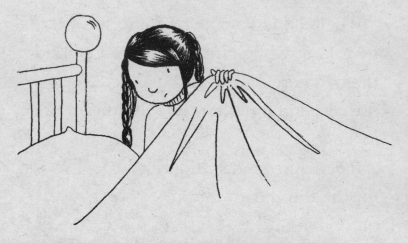

Kirsty tiptoed over to the bed and checked under the lumpy blankets, but she didn't find a goblin there, either.

Suddenly, Harriet started fluttering around excitedly, pointing to one of the long curtains that framed the window.

The girls crept forward to have a closer look, then grinned at each other excitedly. There was a goblin-shaped bump behind the curtain!

Hamster Hide-and-Seek!

Kirsty and Rachel looked at each other, wondering what to do. Then Kirsty had an idea. She put her finger to her lips, warning the others to keep quiet. She wasn't sure if the goblin behind the curtain was the one who had captured Twinkle or not, but if he did have the magic hamster, she wanted to catch him off guard. If she could make him jump, she hoped the goblin would loosen his grip on Twinkle, who could wriggle free!

Kirsty crept toward the curtain as quietly as she could. Then, with a sharp jab of her finger, she poked the curtain right where she guessed the goblin's tummy was.

"Ow!" came a surprised shout.

"Caught you!" Kirsty cried, quickly pulling the curtain to the side. "Now give back Twinkle!" But the goblin behind the curtain was

empty-handed. He dodged past Kirsty and ran straight out of the bedroom.

"So that's one goblin . . ." Harriet mused. "But where are the other two?"

As Harriet spoke, Rachel spotted a pair of green goblin feet sticking out from under the bed. She tiptoed back to the toy box and pulled out one of Jamie's rubber snakes. Then she winked at Kirsty and Harriet, and said in a loud voice, "Ooh! I think I just saw a snake! Do the Coopers have a pet snake, too, Kirsty?"

"No," Kirsty said, catching on to Rachel's plan. "It must be a wild one. Look, there it goes, slithering under Jamie's bed! I wonder if it's poisonous?"

Trying her hardest not to giggle, Rachel pushed the rubber snake under Jamie's bed and made a loud hissing noise. Grinning, Harriet flung some red fairy dust after it, and the snake began wriggling farther under the bed all by itself!

With a squeal, the
goblin scrambled
from his hiding
place and rushed
out of the room.
But he wasn't
holding Twinkle,
either.

"That's two
goblins," said Harriet,
sighing. "Where could
the third one be?"

Just then, the girls heard a nervous
laugh coming from inside the closet.
They guessed that the third goblin must
be hiding inside. Since the other two
didn't have Harriet's magic hamster,
this must be the goblin who had
captured Twinkle!

Kirsty and Rachel stood on either side
of the closet, each holding one door
handle. "One . . . two . . . three!" Rachel
mouthed, and they flung the closet doors
open at the same time.

Kirsty's heart pounded as she looked inside the closet, ready to grab little Twinkle. But all she could see were lots of clothes. Was the goblin somewhere else?

But Harriet was pointing at something in the closet. The girls saw that, sticking out between two of Jamie's superhero costumes, was a pointed green nose! The goblin *was* in the closet — he was just well hidden.

Rachel spotted a Native American feathered headdress on the top shelf of the closet, and it gave her an idea. Kirsty and Harriet watched as Rachel pretended to pull out a feather and tickle the goblin's feet with it.

Harriet had to put a hand over her mouth to keep from laughing at the idea. Nodding excitedly, she waved her wand over the headdress. A large red feather glimmered with a sparkly light, and then leaped out of its place. The feather flew down toward the goblin's toes, and began to tickle them all over!

"Ooh! Ahh! Ooh, stop that!" the goblin giggled, hopping from one foot to another. "Ooh! Ha-ha! Stop it! Hee-hee!"

The feather kept tickling, until the goblin was breathless with laughter. Finally, he couldn't stand it anymore. "Stop!" he roared, between laughs. "Stop!"

"Not until you give back Twinkle!" Rachel and Kirsty both said firmly.

Nibbles Is Nowhere

The goblin's hands appeared through the clothes. A tiny fairy-size Twinkle sat in his cupped palms. "Here — take it! Take it!" the goblin urged. "Just stop the tickling!"

Harriet flew over and scooped up Twinkle. She dropped a kiss on the hamster's little head, then waved her

wand toward the goblin's feet. Red fairy
dust swirled around the feather again. It
glowed brightly and leaped back into its
place in Jamie's headdress.

The goblin jumped out of the closet
and bolted through the bedroom door.
"It's not fair! They were tickling me,"
the girls heard him moan to the
other goblins.

Rachel and Kirsty smiled at each other, then bent to pet little Twinkle. One hamster was safe, at least!

"Now we just have to find Nibbles," Rachel said. "I wonder where he could have gone."

Twinkle was already twitching her nose and looking up at Harriet in a meaningful way. The fairy paid close attention, then nodded at her pet. "Twinkle says she thinks that Nibbles is somewhere up above us in the house," she told Rachel and Kirsty.

"In the attic?" Kirsty asked. "Wow, he's climbed a lot today!"

"Come on, let's find him right away," Rachel said, "before he goes off on another adventure!"

Kirsty, Rachel, and Harriet all rushed up the last staircase to the attic door. But as soon as they stepped inside, all three of them gasped.

"Oh, no!" Kirsty cried, looking around. The small room was stuffed with boxes, suitcases, old furniture, wooden trunks, dusty photo albums, and trinkets, dimly lit by the light that streamed in through a tiny round window. "How are we ever going to find Nibbles in here?"

Luckily, Twinkle seemed to know exactly where to find Nibbles. She

scampered through the air toward a stack
of travel souvenirs. Rachel could see
carved wooden masks, a silk parasol, a
jewelry box piled high with strings of
beads, and even an old brass oil lamp!

Rachel followed
Twinkle,
laughing. "I
was just
thinking that
it's like
Aladdin's
cave up
here," she
said, "and
look! There's
Aladdin's lamp!"
Twinkle seemed interested in the lamp,
too. She pushed at it with her nose, then

looked up at Harriet, her little black
eyes bright.

Rachel carefully lifted the lid of the
lamp and everyone
peeked inside.
There, curled
up and fast
asleep, was
Nibbles!

"Oh, look!"
Rachel said,
dropping her
voice to a whisper
so she wouldn't wake
the sleeping hamster. "How cute. He's
worn out after all his adventures!"

Kirsty gently scooped the sleepy
hamster out of the lamp, feeling relieved.
Now all they had to do was put Nibbles

back in his cage with some fresh food, and clean up the living room. Then everything would be right again.

But just as they were heading toward the door, Kirsty and Rachel heard goblin footsteps pounding up the attic

stairs! The girls looked around quickly for a way to escape, but there was only one door and the tiny window. The goblins were coming — and the friends were trapped!

Happy Hamster

"Quick, Harriet!" Rachel cried. "Fly out the window and take Twinkle home to Fairyland before the goblins can get their hands on her again."

"Yes," Kirsty agreed eagerly. "The goblins won't hang around here once they know you and Twinkle have left."

Harriet nodded, clutching her pet
protectively. "OK. Thank you both for
all your help," she
added, zooming over
to the window. Then
she stopped on the
windowsill, as if
she'd just
remembered
something. "But
before I go, I'd
better clean up the
mess downstairs."

Her wand was
a bright blur as
Harriet waved it in a
complicated pattern, sending
glittering fairy dust spiraling
through the door. "There!" she said.

"And thank you again, girls," she added, hugging them good-bye. "You've both been such a big help!"

"Good-bye Harriet! Good-bye Twinkle!" Rachel and Kirsty said quickly. The goblin footsteps were growing closer by the second!

Harriet fluttered out through the open window just as the three goblins clattered into the attic.

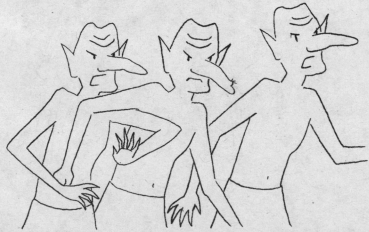

"Follow that fairy!" the first goblin
shouted, spotting the last traces of fairy
magic around the window.

"She's outside. Quick, after her,"
the second one shouted, turning around
so fast that he bumped into the third
goblin.

"Hey! Watch where you're going!"
snapped the third goblin, turning to hurry
back down the attic stairs.

"Well, it's your fault that the hamster got away," Kirsty and Rachel heard one of the other goblins telling him as they all stomped away.

"My fault?" came the indignant reply, drifting faintly up the stairs.

The goblins were soon out of earshot, so Rachel and Kirsty ran over to the attic window to see if they could spot them in the yard. A few minutes later, the three goblins appeared outside, bickering noisily about which way Harriet had gone.

A sparrow suddenly flew across the yard, and one of the goblins pointed excitedly at it. "There's the fairy!" he shouted. The silly goblins chased eagerly after the sparrow as it darted over the back fence and into the meadow.

Back in the attic, Nibbles opened his
eyes and gazed
around as if he was
surprised to find
himself there.

"Hello, Nibbles,"
Kirsty said, petting him
gently. "Let's get you something to eat.
You've had quite the adventure today!"

The girls headed back downstairs and
saw that Harriet had worked her
wonderful fairy magic, as promised. The
living room was spotless!

"Wow!" said Rachel with a grin.
"You'd never guess that this room was
full of wood shavings and hamster toys
just a few minutes ago!"

As Kirsty put Nibbles back into his
cage, she couldn't help smiling. Harriet

hadn't just taken care of the messy living room, she'd also magically filled up Nibbles's bowl with a large helping of sunflower seeds! "His favorite food," Kirsty said, watching the hamster chow down. "Harriet is so smart!"

Kirsty carefully shut the cage door and watched the happy little hamster for a few minutes. "You know, I think I'll take Nibbles back to my house with us," she said. "Just so we know for sure that he's safe from any goblins."

"Good idea," Rachel said. "Then Nibbles will get a little vacation, too."

Kirsty carefully carried the hamster cage over to the door.

"Phew," Rachel said with a sigh, as she and Kirsty left the Coopers' house. "That was a busy morning!" She smiled at her friend. "What could possibly happen tomorrow?"

Kirsty grinned. "I don't know," she replied happily. "But I can't wait to find out!"

Twinkle is back wih Harriet the
Hamster Fairy. Now can Rachel and
Kirsty help

Molly the
Goldfish Fairy

find her fish, Flash?

Gnome, Sweet Gnome

"Slow down, Dad," Kirsty Tate called.
"You're leaving us behind!"

"Sorry." Mr. Tate stopped and waited
for Kirsty, Rachel, and Mrs. Tate to
catch up. "I'm hungry, and you know
how good the Wainwrights' barbecues
always are. In fact . . ." He sniffed the

air. "I think I can smell the food cooking from here!"

"We're still two blocks away!" Kirsty said, grinning and shaking her head. Her best friend Rachel burst out laughing.

Mr. and Mrs. Tate continued walking, and the girls followed.

"We'll have a good time at the barbecue," Kirsty said, smiling. Rachel was staying with her over Easter vacation. "The Wainwrights have a huge yard. It's great."

"Cool!" Rachel said eagerly. Then she lowered her voice. "But don't forget, we have to keep our eyes open for fairy pets, too!"

Kirsty nodded. "The fairies are depending on us," she whispered. "We've

found five pets," Kirsty said as they
turned onto the Wainwrights' street.

"Yes, we just have the goldfish and the
pony left to find," Rachel said
thoughtfully. "The goldfish will be tricky,
though. It's the smallest pet we've had to
look for!"

Fairyland is never far away!
Look for these other

books:

The Rainbow Fairies

#1: Ruby the Red Fairy

#2: Amber the Orange Fairy

#3: Sunny the Yellow Fairy

#4: Fern the Green Fairy

#5: Sky the Blue Fairy

#6: Inky the Indigo Fairy

#7: Heather the Violet Fairy

The Weather Fairies

#1: Crystal the Snow Fairy

#2: Abigail the Breeze Fairy

#3: Pearl the Cloud Fairy

#4: Goldie the Sunshine Fairy

#5: Evie the Mist Fairy

#6: Storm the Lightning Fairy

#7: Hayley the Rain Fairy

The Jewel Fairies

#1: India the Moonstone Fairy

#2: Scarlett the Garnet Fairy

#3: Emily the Emerald Fairy

#4: Chloe the Topaz Fairy

#5: Amy the Amethyst Fairy

#6: Sophie the Sapphire Fairy

#7: Lucy the Diamond Fairy

Special Editions

Joy the Summer Vacation Fairy

Holly the Christmas Fairy

Fairy Friends Sticker Book

Fairy Fashion Dress-up Book

The Pet Fairies

#1: Katie the Kitten Fairy

#2: Bella the Bunny Fairy

#3: Georgia the Guinea Pig Fairy

#4: Lauren the Puppy Fairy

#5: Harriet the Hamster Fairy

And coming soon . . .

#6: Molly the Goldfish Fairy

#7: Penny the Pony Fairy